40

Monster and Frog *Mind The Baby*

ROSE IMPEY

Illustrated by
Jonathan Allen

Collins
A Division of HarperCollins*Pu*

First published in Great Britain by HarperCollins Publishers Ltd in 1994
10 9 8 7 6 5 4 3 2 1
ISBN: 0 00 198052 1
First published in Picture Lions in 1994
Picture Lions is an imprint of the Children's Division, part of HarperCollins Publishers Limited,
77-85 Fulham Palace Road, Hammersmith, London W6 8JB
10 9 8 7 6 5 4 3 2 1
ISBN: 0 00 664341-8
Text copyright © Rose Impey 1994 Illustrations copyright © Jonathan Allen 1994
The author and illustrator assert the moral right to be identified as the author and illustrator of the work.
Produced by HarperCollins Hong Kong. This book is set in 16/24 EduGaramond

Monster's sister had to go out. She asked
Monster to mind the baby. Monster had
never been asked to mind a baby before.

"Don't worry," said Monster's sister, "this baby doesn't cry. She will probably sleep until I get back."

"Hmmm," thought Monster. Minding babies sounded very easy.

Monster tiptoed around the house.

He didn't want to wake the baby.

But suddenly the doorbell rang.
In came Monster's best friend, Frog.
The baby began to cry.
"Hello," said Frog. "What's going on here?"
"Oh, no," said Monster. "You have woken
the baby."
"Don't worry," said Frog. "I know all about
babies." Frog knew all about everything.

"You should pick her up," he said.
"Babies like to be held."
"Do they?" said Monster. "I've never
held a baby before."
Neither had Frog, but he didn't tell
Monster that.
"There's nothing to it," said Frog.
Monster picked up the baby,
very carefully.
"Oh dear," said Monster.
"This baby is wet."

"You should change her nappy," said Frog.
"That's why she's crying."
"Oh," said Monster. He had never changed
a nappy before, either.

"There's nothing to it," said Frog. "Leave it to me. I am an expert on nappies." Monster found a pile of clean nappies. Frog tried to wrap the baby in one. She looked like a parcel.

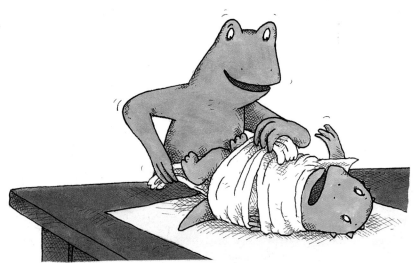

"I don't think that's right," said Monster.

"I was just practising," said Frog.

Frog tried again, but now the baby looked
as if she had been in an accident.
"I don't think that's right, either," said Monster.
"Nappies are not as easy as they look,"
said Frog. There were nappies everywhere.
Frog was having a fight with one.
"I will look in my book," said Monster,
'How to fold a nappy'.

Frog and Monster tried lots of
different ways to fold a nappy.
At last they found a way that
worked. But even a clean nappy
didn't stop the baby from crying.
"That's funny," said Monster.
"This baby doesn't cry."

"I know what's wrong," said Frog. "This
baby is hungry. You should feed her."
"Oh," said Monster. He had never fed
a baby before.
"There's nothing to it," said Frog.
"What do babies eat?" asked Monster.
"Lots of things," said Frog vaguely.

Frog didn't seem to be an expert
on what babies eat. So Monster
looked it up in his book,
'How to feed your baby'.
Monster boiled some milk
and made the baby a bottle.

The baby drank the bottle until it was dry.
But then the baby started to cry again.
"I don't understand," said Monster. "This
baby does *not* cry."

"This baby has wind," said Frog. "You should
put her over your shoulder and pat her
on the back."

"Really?" said Monster.

"Yes," said Frog. "Trust me. There is nothing
I don't know about babies."

Monster picked up the baby, put her over
his shoulder and patted her on the back.
The baby cried louder still.
"Not so hard," said Frog. "You have
to be gentle with babies."

Monster patted, but not so hard this time.
The baby gave a loud burp. The baby
smiled and that made Monster smile too.
At last the baby was quiet – but not for long.

"Oh, dear," said Monster.
"Minding babies is not
as easy as it sounds."

"I know what's wrong," said Frog.
"This baby is bored."

"Bored?" said Monster.

"Yes," said Frog. "Babies like
to play."

"Oh," said Monster. He had never
played with a baby before.

"There's nothing to it," said Frog.
"Watch me."

First Frog tickled
the baby's tummy.

Then he rocked the baby's cradle.
Then he sang to the baby, but
this made the baby cry more.

Then Frog played Peek-a-boo with the
baby, but this made the baby jump.
She cried even louder.

"Let me try," said Monster.
He picked the baby up.
First Monster pulled funny
faces to make the baby smile.

Then he gave the baby
a ride on his knee.

Then he did a little dance with the baby. Monster did everything he could think of, but the baby *still* cried. Monster looked as if *he* was about to cry too.

"Don't worry," said Frog, "I will think of something. I am full of ideas."
But the baby was heavy and Monster was tired. He put the baby back to bed. There was something in the bed.

"What's this?" asked Monster.

"That is a dummy," said Frog.

"What is it for?" said Monster.

"Babies suck them," said Frog,

"to stop them from crying."

"Really?" said Monster.

"Yes," said Frog. "I know all about dummies. Leave it to me."

Frog put the dummy in the baby's
mouth and straightaway the baby
stopped crying. The baby fell fast asleep.
Suddenly the house was very quiet.
Monster and Frog were afraid to move.
They didn't want to wake the baby up.

Just then Monster's sister
came home.
"Look at my baby," said
Monster's sister.
"She is so good. Give her
a dummy and she sleeps
all the time."

"Yes," said Frog. "That is just what I told
Monster. It's a good job I was here.
Babies are my speciality."